Max's Trip

Level 5B

Written by Melanie Hamm
Illustrated by Kate Daubney
Reading Consultant: Betty Franchi

About Phonics

Spoken English uses more than 40 speech sounds. Each sound is called a *phoneme*. Some phonemes relate to a single letter (d-o-g) and others to combinations of letters (sh-ar-p). When a phoneme is written down, it is called a *grapheme*. Teaching these sounds, matching them to their written form, and sounding out words for reading is the basis of phonics.

Early phonics instruction gives children the tools to sound out, blend, and say the words without having to rely on memory or guesswork. This instruction gives children the confidence and ability to read unfamiliar words, helping them progress toward independent reading.

About the Consultant

Betty Franchi is an American educator with a Bachelor's Degree in Elementary and Middle Education as well as a Master's Degree in Special Education. Betty holds a National Boards for Professional Teaching Standards certification. Throughout her 24 years as a teacher, she has studied and developed an expertise in Phonetic Awareness and has implemented phonetic strategies, teaching many young children to read, including students with special needs.

Reading tips

This book focuses on the *d* sound
(made with the letters *ed*) as in rain**ed**.

Tricky and/or new words in this book

Any words in bold may have unusual spellings
or are new and have not yet been introduced.

> **Tricky and/or new words in this book**
>
> **foxes   desert**

Extra ways to have fun with this book

After the readers have finished the story, ask them
questions about what they have just read.

What did Max see from the hot-air balloon?
Can you remember two words that contain
the d sound shown by the letters ed?

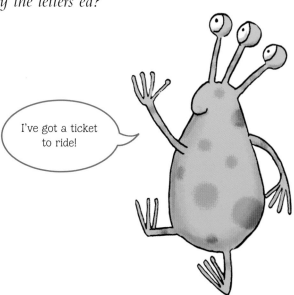

I've got a ticket
to ride!

A Pronunciation Guide

This grid contains the sounds used in the stories in levels 4, 5, and 6 and a guide on how to say them.

/ă/ as in pat	/ā/ as in pay	/âr/ as in care	/ä/ as in father
/b/ as in bib	/ch/ as in church	/d/ as in deed/ milled	/ĕ/ as in pet
/ē/ as in bee	/f/ as in fife/ phase/ rough	/g/ as in gag	/h/ as in hat
/hw/ as in which	/ĭ/ as in pit	/ī/ as in pie/ by	/îr/ as in pier
/j/ as in judge	/k/ as in kick/ cat/ pique	/l/ as in lid/ needle (nēd'l)	/m/ as in mom
/n/ as in no/ sudden (sŭd'n)	/ng/ as in thing	/ŏ/ as in pot	/ō/ as in toe
/ô/ as in caught/ paw/ for/ horrid/ hoarse	/oi/ as in noise	/o͝o/ as in took	/ū/ as in cute

/ou/ as in out	/p/ as in pop	/r/ as in roar	/s/ as in sauce
/sh/ as in ship/ dish	/t/ as in tight/ stopped	/th/ as in thin	/th/ as in this
/ŭ/ as in cut	/ûr/ as in urge/ term/ firm/ word/ heard	/v/ as in valve	/w/ as in with
/y/ as in yes	/z/ as in zebra/ xylem	/zh/ as in vision/ pleasure/ garage/	/ə/ as in about/ item/ edible/ gallop/ circus
/ər/ as in butter			

Be careful not to add an /uh/ sound to /s/, /t/, /p/, /c/, /h/, /r/, /m/, /d/, /g/, /l/, /f/ and /b/. For example, say /fff/ not /fuh/ and /sss/ not /suh/.

Max was off on a trip. He grabbed his bags and his ticket.

He was so excited, he didn't
even mind if it rained.

Max gave his ticket to the pilot.
He climbed into the hot-air balloon

'Off we go!" he called.

They hovered over the hills.
Max saw rivers and trees and shee

They moved across a jungle.
Max saw tigers and lions and snakes.

They raced over a forest.
Max saw deer and bears and **foxe**

In the middle of the sea,
it rained. Max saw waves
and ships and sharks.

They went to the **desert**.
Max saw sand and camels
and a rocket.

Max frowned and shrugged.
'3, 2, 1, blastoff!"
yelled the pilot.

They took off and flew
to the Moon.

Max saw dust and rocks and aliens!
He grabbed the pilot, "Let's go!"

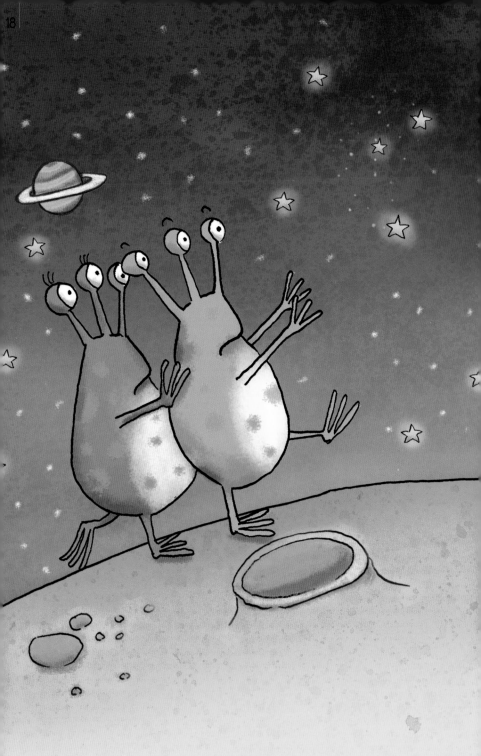

The aliens chased them back
to the rocket.

"Quick! Get inside," cried the pilot.
He opened the door.

"Let us in!" bellowed the aliens.
"Look, we have tickets."
They showed the pilot.

"Okay," smiled the pilot.
'All aboard!"

Back at Max's house,
the aliens had dinner.

They liked it so much,
they stayed for a week.

OVER **48** TITLES IN SIX LEVELS
Betty Franchi recommends...

Other titles to enjoy from Level 4

The Maze — I love reading phonics — 978 1 84898 771 5

Fairy Fay's Bad Day — I love reading phonics — 978 1 84898 772 2

Eve the Knight — I love reading phonics — 978 1 84898 773 9

Some titles from Level 5

Snapped by Sam! — I love reading phonics — 978 1 84898 775 3

George the Genius Gerbil — I love reading phonics — 978 1 84898 777 7

Budge Troll, Budge! — I love reading phonics — 978 1 84898 778 4

Some titles from Level 6

What Wally Wanted — I love reading phonics — 978 1 84898 779 1

Superhero Ed! — I love reading phonics — 978 1 84898 780 7

The Robot Bop — I love reading phonics — 978 1 84898 782 1

An Hachette Company
First Published in the United States by TickTock, an imprint of Octopus Publishing Group.
www.octopusbooksusa.com

Copyright © Octopus Publishing Group Ltd 2013

Distributed in the US by
Hachette Book Group USA
237 Park Avenue, New York NY 10017, USA

Distributed in Canada by
Canadian Manda Group
165 Dufferin Street, Toronto, Ontario, Canada M6K 3H6

ISBN 978 1 84898 776 0

Printed and bound in China
10 9 8 7 6 5 4 3 2 1